Hamster Holmes

COMBING FOR CLUES

By **Albin Sadar**

Illustrated by **Valerio Fabbretti**

Ready-to-Read

Simon Spotlight

New York London Toronto Sydney New Delhi

To my beautiful and precious
little bunny — A. S.

SIMON SPOTLIGHT
An imprint of Simon & Schuster Children's Publishing Division
1230 Avenue of the Americas, New York, New York 10020
This Simon Spotlight edition September 2015
Text copyright © 2015 by Albin Sadar
Illustrations copyright © 2015 by Valerio Fabbretti
For information about special discounts for bulk purchases, please contact Simon & Schuster
Special Sales at 1-866-506-1949 or business@simonandschuster.com.
Manufactured in the United States of America 0715 LAK
10 9 8 7 6 5 4 3 2 1
Library of Congress Cataloging-in-Publication Data
Sadar, Albin.
Hamster Holmes, combing for clues / by Albin Sadar ; illustrated by Valerio Fabbretti.
pages cm. — (Hamster Holmes ; 2) (Ready-to-read. Level 2)
Summary: "Hamster Holmes and Dr. Watt want to help their friend Ouchy the porcupine find his
missing comb, but have trouble finding clues. Can a comb vanish into thin air?"— Provided by
publisher.
ISBN 978-1-4814-2039-6 (pb : alk. paper) — ISBN 978-1-4814-2040-2 (hc : alk. paper) —
ISBN 978-1-4814-2041-9 (eBook) [1. Mystery and detective stories. 2. Detectives—Fiction.
3. Hamsters—Fiction. 4. Animals—Fiction.] I. Fabbretti, Valerio, illustrator. II. Title.
III. Title: Combing for clues.
PZ7.1.S23Haj 2015
[E]—dc23
2014048493

Hamster Holmes and
his firefly friend, Dr. Watt,
liked solving mysteries.
In between cases, they did
fun experiments.
"If I mix yellow and blue,"
Hamster Holmes asked Dr. Watt,
"what color will I make?"

Dr. Watt spoke in Morse code.
He blinked his light on and off
to form the dashes and dots
of each letter.
A long flash of light was a dash.
A short flash of light was a dot.

Dr. Watt flashed, "Dash-dash-dot, dot-dash-dot, dot, dot, dash-dot." They mixed the yellow and blue and watched as the color changed. "G-R-E-E-N. Green it is, Dr. Watt!" Hamster Holmes said with a smile. All of a sudden, there was a knock at the door.

It was Ouchy the porcupine.
"I need your help to solve
a mystery," he cried.
"We're on the case, old friend!"
Hamster Holmes looked at Ouchy,
then added, "Does the mystery
have something to do with the park
and your messy quills?"

Ouchy looked surprised.

"How did you know?" he asked.

"I observed," said Hamster Holmes.

"Your paws are coated with a kind
of sand found only in the park!"
Then he explained that, usually,
Ouchy's quills were neatly combed.
But today they looked *quite* messy!

"Very clever," said Ouchy.
"I knew I came to the right place."
Dr. Watt nodded.
"I didn't comb my quills today,"
Ouchy continued, "because I lost
my favorite comb in the park.
I put it down for a second,
and it vanished!"

Hamster Holmes grabbed his
special detective coat and said,
"Then to the park we shall go!
Come along, Dr. Watt.
The game is on!"

At the park, Ouchy showed them
where he last saw his comb.
"It was on this bench, where I
always comb my quills after I walk."
Using his magnifying glass,
Hamster Holmes looked at the seat.
"Hmm . . . I don't see any clues,"
he said.

Dr. Watt looked under the bench,
using his light to help him see.
He didn't find any clues, either.
"Where else did you go?"
Hamster Holmes asked Ouchy.
"It might help if we follow in
your footsteps."
Ouchy thought hard for a moment.

He led them to the water fountain.
"I always stop for a drink of water
before I walk around the park,"
he explained.
Hamster Holmes and Dr. Watt
didn't find any clues there, either.
But they weren't about to give up!

"If you walked around the park,
we need to do the same thing!"
said Hamster Holmes.
So he, Ouchy, and Dr. Watt went
everywhere Ouchy had walked.
Still they did not find any clues.

Next Hamster Holmes asked Ouchy
to describe his missing comb
in detail so Dr. Watt could
make a sketch.

"It has a white handle and is shaped a bit like a fish," began Ouchy.
Dr. Watt looked confused.
He had never heard of a comb shaped like a fish!

"I know that sounds unusual,
but it is a very special comb,"
Ouchy explained. "It belonged
to my great-grandfather,
Ouchy the First," he said proudly.
It had been passed down to every
Ouchy in the family.

"It sounds very special indeed," said Hamster Holmes.
Dr. Watt agreed, and he put the finishing touches on his sketch.

"Does your comb look like this?"
Hamster Holmes asked,
showing the sketch to Ouchy.
"Amazing!" said Ouchy.
"It looks just like that except
the comb part is gold."
Hamster Holmes began to wonder
if the comb was not lost at all.

He wondered if it was stolen!
"Was anyone in the park who might
have been a witness?" he asked.
"We'll want to interview them."
Ouchy thought for a second.
He said he saw Annie Bunny
and Hickory Hedgehog.

They found the hedgehog nearby.
"May we ask you some questions,
Mr. Hedgehog?" Hamster Holmes
asked.
They showed him the sketch.
"Sorry. I haven't seen it,"
Hickory said, crossing his arms.
Dr. Watt pointed at Hickory's hair.
It looked neatly combed.

Hamster Holmes raised his eyebrows.

"I know what you're thinking," said Hickory. "But I assure you, I did not take that comb! I keep my hair short, so it never gets tangled," he said proudly. "I have no use for combs."

They moved on to the next witness, Annie Bunny.

She hadn't seen the comb either, but she wanted to help.

"Try asking Josiah Mutt, the old dog who spends most days in the park. Maybe he saw something fishy!"

Hamster Holmes cracked a smile.
He liked a good joke.
He also liked a witness with
a good lead.
Sure enough, the dog was
digging nearby.

"Excuse me, Mr. Mutt. I'd like to
have a word," Hamster Holmes said.
"You'd like to have a *worm*?"
Josiah replied. "Sorry, but I
can't help you with that.
I like dog food, myself."
Hamster Holmes spoke louder.

"No, I'd like to TALK with you.
Have you seen this COMB?"
The old dog hadn't seen it.
"If you see it, please let us know,"
said Hamster Holmes.
"And if you see a nice BONE,
let me know," Josiah said.
"I collect them!"

It seemed like a dead end.
Hamster Holmes went for a run
on the wheel to help him think.
But it was Dr. Watt who had an idea.
He flashed a word in Morse code
and pointed at Ouchy's quills.
"You spelled W-H-Y? Why?"
Hamster Holmes asked. "Oh, I see!"

Dr. Watt nodded.

"Ouchy," Hamster Holmes began, "you said you always get water, then walk around the park, then comb your quills. But today, your quills are messy. *Why* did you put down your comb if you hadn't used it yet?"

Ouchy explained that he was
just about to comb his hair when
he saw an ice-cream cart.
He put down his comb,
ran to get an ice pop,
and went for a stroll while he ate.
"Then what happened?" asked
Hamster Holmes.

"Hmm . . . ," said Ouchy, "when I came back, Josiah was digging. I forgot about that!"

"Was he *digging*, or was he covering something?" asked Hamster Holmes. They walked over to Josiah and asked to see his bone collection.

Josiah dug up all kinds of things,
but only a few bones.
Suddenly, Hamster Holmes yelled
for him to stop digging and said,
"The mystery is . . . solved!"
He held up Ouchy's comb.
Josiah had buried it by mistake,
thinking it was a fish bone!

Josiah apologized, but Ouchy was just happy to have his comb back! "Josiah, old chap, perhaps it is time to get new spectacles," Hamster Holmes told him. *"Popsicles?"* Josiah asked. "Thanks, but cold food hurts my teeth."

The next day, to thank everyone, Ouchy returned with a surprise. "I smell treats!" Josiah shouted, before the box was opened. "Your sense of smell is amazing!" Hamster Holmes told Josiah. "Next time we need to track a scent for a case, we'd love your help!"